The Heir and the Spare

A Historical Regency Romance Novel

By

Sara November

Copyright © 2017

Dunnmade Books

All Rights Reserved.

This book or individual parts may not be reproduced or transmitted without written permission from the publisher regardless of format.

Introduction:

Edmund Templeton is the second son of a prominent Duke. His net worth is roughly ninety thousand pounds. When we meet him in the beginning of the story, he's prodigal and on a mission to squander his life fortune gambling and drinking. He's a womanizer who doesn't know his father has just engaged him to an Earl's daughter. This is an engagement he's absolutely desperate to get out of. Lavinia is the new governess at the Duke's house. Unknowingly she has captivated Edmund's attention at first sight. She's improperly brash and can't seem to resist an opportunity to rile Edmund, who's aware of his growing attraction for her. At the masquerade ball hosted by the Duke, he proposes marriage to her, catching her entirely by surprise.

Both Edmund and Lavinia stand to gain as well as lose by this marriage of convenience. Will they go ahead with it? Will they learn new things about each other in the process? Who will get in their way, and who will help them along?

Read on to find more.

Table of Contents

[Chapter 1](#) 1

[Chapter 2](#) 10

[Chapter 3](#) 18

[Chapter 4](#) 27

[Chapter 5](#) 34

[Chapter 6](#) 42

Chapter 1

1812 Courtney Hall, Yorkshire.

Edmund Templeton was in the library when she called. His butler had come in to declare that a young lady sought audience with Lord Templeton. Edmund had no idea who the lady was or what she wanted with his father. Nevertheless, he asked Albert to let her in. In the absence of both his father and his brother James, he was the lord of the house and it would in no way be a breach of etiquette to hear her out.

When she entered the library, Edmund knew he was in trouble. Dark brown locks framed her alluring face, her jet black pupils dared him to look. Her dowdy style of dress instantly suggested she was not of the aristocracy. Her stance suggested an unwarranted confidence. She was so unfazed by the Lord's luxuries that Edmund was taken aback.

"Sir," she curtsied, her body suppliant but her eyes still looking at him haughtily, as though she knew the entire ritual was of no consequence. More importantly, she knew he was no Duke himself, but the second son.

"Pray tell me your name, young woman, and your purpose for being here."

"Lavinia. His Lordship wished to interview me for the post of governess to Mr. James Templeton's ward."

"Yes, I do remember father and James discussing the need for a competent governess for young Henrietta. They have gone hunting, and should be back in about… he paused to check his fob watch, and continued, "two hours. If you wouldn't mind, you can wait in the salon outside."

"The butler could have directed me as much. I wonder why I was called to you."

Impertinence! While the same words might've been considered banter coming from a high-born woman, from her they were a serious breach of propriety. Edmund wondered whether she would care if he chose to make it known to her as such.

"We don't see young ladies of no consequence seeking interviews with His Lordship very often, so it was mere curiosity that made me invite you in."

"And has your curiosity been sated?"

"That depends on the original extent of the curiosity, doesn't it? Leave it to my judgment to decide whether I'm sated, and kindly wait outside."

"No, sir. Your curiosity has now whetted mine, and I shall not rest until I am satisfied."

Edmund's patience was running out with every impertinent remark of hers. He wasn't a patient man to start with, which was the chief reason his father trusted James with the running of the estate.

"It is not my duty to answer your absurd questions. Please see yourself out, or I would be forced to call my footman."

"You'd be wasting your time."

Without further thought, Edmund rang for Albert. The challenge in her eyes was unabated.

"Yes, Master Templeton?"

"Please escort Miss Lavinia into the salon."

"You cannot touch me, Alfred. I do not wish to go. My appointment with Mr. Templeton here is not over. You may leave."

"Impudent woman! You dare to order my own butler in my house?"

"Not your butler, Mr. Templeton. But your father's. I don't understand why aristocrats forget that."

"I'll have you know, disrespectful woman, that any man in my position would've either beaten you soundly or thrown you physically out of the house."

"Physical violence is the best your kind can do, anyway."

"My kind? How many sons of Dukes have you even met in your life, you lowly wretch?"

"Enough. Enough for a lifetime. Far too many."

With that, she went out of the library with an abruptness that shocked Edmund quite as much as her initial refusal had.

No man or woman, high-bred or not, had ever dared to insult him so openly anywhere, let alone in his own house. He'd had his fair share of mutually provoked fights, but this had stung too deep to allow for easy redress. The woman would have hell to pay.

The woman, too, was hardly in a state of less turmoil. She hadn't meant her true feelings for the aristocracy to become apparent this easily, for when all was said and done, she did need the position of governess. It galled her that Templeton's son would become an obstacle in her path, but since all the obstacle-creating had been her doing, she couldn't be too captious. She only hoped that the Lord Templeton didn't set too much store by his wayward rake of a younger son.

She was sitting in the salon, like she had always intended to, despite what she had said to Templeton. But entitled rakes like him never ceased to tempt her into riling them up. It wasn't just rakes either; she had a profound dislike for anyone related to the aristocracy, particularly the males who thought of their father's wealth as their own. Templeton had so far been a perfect match.

An hour passed, and the salon didn't become any more occupied. She found that odd, given how grand houses such as Courtney Hall tended to be bustling with people: grooms, butlers, maids, footmen, members of the family...but Courtney was about as bleak as the Yorkshire moors on which it was situated. The Templetons were not famous as a family, but their younger son Edmund Templeton had often caused scandal, dragging the family name into the periodicals. He had been known to impregnate women (both noble and common) and make bare knuckle boxing opponents bleed to death. He had a fascination with hearing nose bones snap. On any given day he could be found frequenting clubs and gambling away great portions of his inheritance. Templeton was notoriously known to commit a litany of misdemeanors Lavinia didn't care to call to mind. The accidental pregnancies had for the most part been kept secret, but Lavinia knew about them from the time she was a private nurse and had attended to a growing number of women across counties. The thing that drove her the maddest was the number of unfortunate women she had seen die mid childbirth simply because of some Duke or Earl's uncontrollable sex wand. With the other vices at least, both parties stood to lose equally. But she had never heard of a man die after an ill-considered affair.

The other two Templeton men were back not long after, and the Duke invited Lavinia into his study. Edmund was already positioned within an earshot.

"Miss Lavinia, I understand that you're offering your services as Henrietta's governess," the Duke began.

Edmund had a strong desire to tell his father what had transpired in the library, but he resisted. He had no wish to see the odious woman live under his roof on a regular basis, although she was being more compliant with his father. Her conciliating tone and countenance were much more becoming to her than her earlier haughtiness had been, and he wondered if he had wronged her in some particular way to have put her on the offensive like that.

While she and her father were negotiating the terms of her employment, he thought back to all the women he had bedded without affording them the courtesy of remembering their face. Had Lavinia perhaps been one of them? No, had he ever gone to bed with her, he would've remembered that unforgettable wench. He had known her all of two hours, and he still felt inexplicably drawn.

Once Lavinia had left, Lord Templeton announced that he wanted to have a private conversation with Edmund. He always dreaded such meetings with his father, for their content was mind-numbingly predictable. The Duke would advise him to not indulge in boxing, whoring, gambling and drinking. He would typically threaten to cut his inheritance and allowance if Edmund didn't comply. If Edmund undertook his advice everything would remain untouched..

Edmund hadn't been out all day so he was anxious to feel the cold December air fondle his face as he rode through the moors.

"Father, could we please have this conversation on the morrow?"

"No, Edmund, I'm afraid not. It is a matter of gravest consequence."

Edmund wondered which of his offenses he was going to list; could father have received word about the fifteen thousand pounds he lost gambling last Thursday or the way he beat up Thomas Piddleworth at Friday's match.

"I've consented to giving your hand in marriage to a most eligible young woman."

Edmund, who was in the business of shocking other people, felt his jaw drop. "You've arranged my marriage? Without my permission?"

"Might I remind you that it is you who are in the position of seeking my permission and not the other way around?"

"But why? I'm all of twenty two!" he said, his voice growing hoarse with indignation.

"That is precisely why. Only twenty-two, and you've already squandered twenty times your allowance this week!"

"And you thought the best way to punish me for my...profligacy... is to marry me off to some female I don't even know?"

"Tell me, Edmund. Would it be considered capital punishmentto saddle you? He who doesn't deal with same female for longer than a night, with someone for life? To give someone as irresponsible as you a family? For whose welfare you would be solely responsible?"

The Duke hadn't reached where he was by being kind that had always been clear to Edmund. Yet he had been happy so long as his father's wiles were directed at some other party.

"I don't agree to this father. I will not marry....whatever her name is."

"Oh but you will. She is Cassandra Wycliff, the daughter of the Earl of Cumbria. I will print the engagement in the papers tomorrow."

Edmund wanted to scream, rage, protest against his impossible father, but since he was the spare and not the heir, he had no power.

"Had I been the heir to the Dukedom, would you still have treated me the same?"

"Of course not. You would then have been married when you were eighteen. I've spared you this long because your frivolous activities don't affect the estate. Much."

"Then why put me to the torture rack now?"

"Because they do affect the estate, however minuscule the effect might be. As my son, you're expected to help the Dukedom grow, not drain its wealth for your personal hedonism."

"Would you let me meet this Wycliff woman once?"

"By all means, if you intend to bed her. That would put the seal on this union for good, and you wouldn't be able to retreat," the Duke said with a roguish smile.

"I could also leave her at the altar and cause scandal."

"My dear, dear boy. That would be the last scandal you would ever cause, for you'd stop being Edmund Templeton after that. The last I checked, polite society doesn't really care about the lives of butlers. Or footmen. And I'm being kind here. Peers don't hire men such as you even as footmen."

It was then that Edmund knew he had been well and truly cornered. "Very well then, father. If your mind is made up, there's precious little I can do."

The Duke had to pinch himself to be certain. "Could you write that down please? You are consenting to the arrangement?"

"I don't have a choice father. And I really don't enjoy the prospect of penury."

"That's the most Templeton thing you've ever said to me, son. May your tribe increase!"

Having appeased his father thus, he set out for the boxing ring. He saw how limited his options were, but he wasn't the notorious buck Edmund Templeton for nothing. It was only a matter of time before a suitable solution came to mind.

On his way, he saw Lavinia out for a walk. He wanted to stop and take a closer look into her piercing eyes, though his spirits weren't jovial enough to justify the way they would sink after. By the time he reached the ring in the village, the rudiments of a plan had begun to form.

Chapter 2

When Lavinia went downstairs for breakfast the next morning, she hadn't expected to hear things that would overturn her entire purpose for being at Courtney Hall. At the servants' table, the footmen as well as the lady's maids couldn't stop giggling. Albert was trying to make them maintain some decorum but in vain.

"What is the matter with all of you this morning?" Albert asked.

"Mr. Collier, I know you've heard of Master Templeton's impending marriage," Rachel, a lady's maid, said.

"But I don't see how such an announcement merits the laughter you lot seem engaged in."

"It doesn't, in all fairness, but I'm certain the maids have a reason to be heartbroken," said Bertram, a particularly cheeky footman.

"I beg your pardon, I'm new here," Lavinia began. "I'm afraid I'm not quite up to speed on whom the marriage is to."

"Worry not, Miss Lavinia. I only heard the particulars myself this morning," Albert said. "The fortunate lady is Miss Wycliff of Cumbria."

Lavinia felt as though someone had stabbed her. She couldn't imagine that happening, for all the justice in the world. This position was the most lucrative and comfortable she had managed to acquire in the last few years, and she couldn't bear the thought of someone like Miss Wycliff of Cumbria ruining it for her.

"Is Miss Wycliff an acquaintance of the family?"

"No, Miss. But I'm given to understand that the Lord's younger son has danced with her at a few masquerade balls in London."

"Pardon me again for being presumptuous, but from what I've heard, Mr. Edmund Templeton isn't known for his inclination to marry," she said tentatively.

"When your father the Duke commands you, I don't suppose you have much choice in the matter," informed Bertram. "But you are right, Mr. Templeton is quite a notorious rake. I'm shocked myself."

"Enough, Bertram. I will not tolerate gossip about the Duke's family at this table," Albert said. The anger in his voice was palpable, which seemed to quiet everyone for a while. But nothing could begin to quiet the storm in Lavinia's mind. She'd been starving, but she hardly ate.

Lavinia was instructing Henrietta in Lord Byron's poetry when there was a knock on the study.

"Come in," the ever-sprightly Henrietta shouted. Edmund came in.

"Good morning, Mr. Templeton. I wonder what brings you to the study at such an hour. You knew your niece would be occupied in her studies."

"I came in to check on her progress."

Lavinia looked at him suspiciously, as though she didn't think an uncle coming in to check on his niece's progress was acceptable.

"You want to check her progress by interrupting it."

Henrietta giggled. "Don't tease uncle so, Miss Lavinia. He is quick to take offense."

"Is he now? But I didn't say anything even remotely flippant, or improper," she smirked, while fixing Edmund with a stare that dared him to recall the previous day in the library. Edmund stood there, transfixed.

"Look at him, Miss," Henrietta smiled. "He's already tongue-tied."

"I'm not tongue-tied Henrietta, thank you very much," he said with a look that made Henrietta decide to stop being impudent. Lavinia could see that while Edmund allowed his niece liberties to poke fun at him, he was also quick to remind her that she was his junior by many, many years.

"Felicitations on your impending nuptials, Mr. Templeton. Rather belated, but my apologies," Lavinia said suddenly.

"Thank you, Miss Lavinia. If only the occasion called for as much felicitation as everyone seems to be directing towards me."

"Why, one would think you would've conveyed your grievances with the match to your esteemed father!"

"I did, but once my father makes his mind up, he's an unpersuadable as I am."

"Do you know why he chose Miss Wycliff? Is Lord Wycliff a particular friend of his?"

It had been so long since Lavinia had seen the Wycliffs that she had no idea who their current friends might be.

"Not to my knowledge, but he does seem to think Cassandra Wycliff a most eligible match for me.

"And what would be your reasons for not being amenable to it, if I could be so presumptuous as to ask?"

Lavinia had phrased it as a request, but Edmund felt it like the force of a command. For the life of him, he couldn't understand why a mere governess had such an impact on him.

"It would be more prudent to discuss this matter when young Henrietta is not listening. Why don't we convene in the grounds after lunch today?"

"Pray tell me, Uncle Edmund. I'm most intrigued!"

"No, Henrietta, certain matters are not fit for the hearing of a young lady of good breeding such as yourself."

"But you are also a young lady of good breeding, Miss Lavinia. Why do you get to hear them?

"I'm ten years your senior. I think that might have something to do with it."

Downstairs, preparations for the first masquerade ball of the season were underway. Lord Templeton had just been in to announce that Courtney Hall was to host it the coming Wednesday.

Lunch was now a markedly different affair, since all the chatter about the marriage had been replaced with chatter about the ball. Lavinia's thoughts, however, were still on Edmund's objections to the match. The servants thought she was feeling overworked at having to teach Henrietta, but that wasn't difficult at all; she was an inquisitive young girl, wiser far beyond her eight years. What occupied her for the entirety of her lunch hour was what she was expecting out of the meeting with Mr. Templeton. Telling him the truth was out of the question, since it would open a veritable Pandora's Box. But she had to find some other way to ensure that the marriage didn't get solemnized. She knew what Cassandra Wycliff was capable of, she didn't need another demonstration.

Edmund didn't go riding that windy afternoon. He strolled the grounds instead, waiting on a promise that Lavinia might not keep. He wasn't clear on why he had requested a private meeting, or what he was expecting her response to be, but it was a ray of hope, and that would have to be enough.

To his delighted surprise, he saw her figure walking towards him.

"Thank you for coming, Miss Lavinia," he said as she curtsied.

"The curiosity was all mine," she said with a slight twitch of her mouth. If Edmund minded, it didn't show on his face. She was certain that any reminder of their mutually discourteous first meeting couldn't delight him, so she took particular pleasure in reminding him of the same.

"I was curious too, Miss Lavinia, as to what particular interest you have in the marriage."

"I happen to have met Miss Wycliff and family, and I can tell you, trusting your utmost confidence, that it wasn't a happy acquaintance."

"So you wish to extract your revenge by ensuring that this marriage does not take place?"

"Not at all, sir. I don't consider myself the vindictive sort, and I would gain nothing by stopping you from a marriage that you might otherwise wish. However, I feel that you don't wish it, so I wondered if I could help you there."

"And how exactly do you propose to help me?"

"By telling you that Cassandra Wycliff is the worst sort of woman anyone can hope to marry."

"But then you would be trying to prevent the marriage."

"Is it in my power to prevent? Did you not say mere hours ago that you're merely acceding to your father's wishes?"

"I am. But if you could find me some evidence of Miss Wycliff's unsuitability, we might still be able to dissuade him."

Evidence was really all it always came down to. She hadn't been able to furnish any the last time, and she was sure she wouldn't be able to do so this time.

"I'm sorry I don't have evidence sir. But I can attempt to locate some in return for a favour."

Edmund knew she had to have something up her sleeve. He didn't think there was any favour that wasn't in his power to grant, so he agreed. Besides, being in her good books was indispensable to his alternative plan.

"All I ask, Mr. Templeton, is that my face never be shown before any of the Wycliffs. Not at the masquerade ball, and certainly not if Miss Wycliff becomes mistress of Courtney."

"Do you fear vendetta at their hands?"

"I cannot tell you that. But please, don't let them see my face."

"At a masquerade ball, such a condition is easily achieved. And I hope Miss Wycliff becoming the mistress of Courtney is still within our powers to avoid."

"I hope so too." Edmund went back to his room, lost in thoughts of what Lavinia could possibly have against Cassandra Wycliff. In what capacity had Lavinia worked under the Earl? Was she governess to Cassandra? What kind of information was Lavinia privy to? Did Cassandra have a child outside wedlock? Was the family's wealth ill-gotten?

Then there was the matter of her wishing to not be seen. Why did she fear recognition at the hands of the family? Did they have enough information on her to ruin her? Had she been mistreated at their hands or was she the culprit herself? What were her motives for revenge?

His brain whirred with questions, but nothing she had said could give him any hint as to what she knew. He would have to be content with the pace at which she chose to tell him, and he wasn't willing to make her desperate by forcing her hand. After all, he had no hope of knowing what Cassandra Wycliff was really like without Lavinia's help.

He took a look at the date. In less than a month, he was going to be married, unless he found a way out. His own plan was extremely risky (and risqué), but he would have to resort to it if Lavinia's help proved insufficient.

Chapter 3

Windermere Castle, Cumbria.

Happy was the day the Countess Cumbria's daughter Cassandra was announced to be engaged to Lord Templeton's younger son. With her elder daughter gone, her only hope for motherly pride was her younger, and Cassandra hadn't disappointed.

"Oh, Cassandra. I knew it. I knew your coming out at Almack's was not in vain. Your pretty face was bound to ensnare some young Duke or Marquis! And with Beau Bummell approving of your fashion choices too!"

"Mother. It was a masquerade ball. So whatever ensnared him was not my face. Besides, he isn't even the Duke's heir. He only gets the estate if his brother dies. Pity, poor old James Templeton is already married."

"Despair not, my child. Edmund Templeton has a fortune of ninety thousand pounds. You would never want for anything."

"But he's an absolute wastrel," Cassandra rolled her eyes. "If he had two hundred thousand pounds it would not matter."

"That's precisely why this marriage is such a great match, my darling. You will keep your fist tight on those pounds so he isn't able to waste them."

Cassandra smiled and said, "I think he wouldn't know what struck him."

Despite her apparent dislike for Edmund, Cassandra was thrilled at being able to dream of being the mistress of Courtney Hall one day. She was the daughter of an Earl, true, but it was a step up to be marrying a Duke's son. She would ideally have loved to marry the Duke himself, but since that wasn't a possibility, she had to be content with what she was getting. Far it be from her to harbour any romantic notions of marriage; she would gladly wed an ogre if it gave her ninety thousand pounds and a comfortable house.

Courtney Hall, Yorkshire.

"A public subscription masquerade ball?" the Duchess asked her husband. "Are you deliberately trying to turn Courtney Hall into a house of ill-repute?"

"No, Tilda. Why must you be so...country about your manners? They are quite the vogue in London, in the bon ton. The best of peers go there, and no one ever calls London a place of ill-repute now, do they?"

"But they are private balls, I'm certain. Inviting the villagers over and giving them free alcohol is asking for riots."

In this, Lord Templeton could not counter his wife. But the ball had been announced, and to retreat now would be to risk ridicule in the county.

"We have placed palace guards all around, Tilda. You can put your mind at ease. No villager would dare to ruin the peace of the Hall."

"I hope you're right, Graham."

The day of the masquerade ball arrived, and a horde of commoners entered the hallowed Courtney Hall. They were dressed as clowns, shepherdesses, animals...whatever suited their fancy.

The Wycliffs were fashionably late, and Cassandra looked around for her prospective fiancé. She had come particularly to get a chance to talk to him and understand how easy or difficult it would be to convince him to involve her in his financial decisions. But given the frivolity and uninhibited joy on display, a rendezvous with him didn't seem likely.

Lavinia, on the other hand, had dressed in a light blue gown with a royal blue mask on her face, keen to explore what people were doing but equally keen to avoid detection. She didn't need to see Cassandra's face to know that the woman in golden brown curls and black gown was her.

The master of ceremonies directed the music to a waltz, and Lavinia found herself face to face with a tall gentleman clad in green breeches.

"Evening, young lady. I don't know who you are, but that gown suits your figure very well," he said while clasping her waist.

Lavinia thanked heavens for the mask, for she was blushing furiously underneath. With a jolt, she realized that the voice belonged to Templeton, which made her blush even redder. She dared not say anything, so she just nodded.

"I see. You're afraid to say something because you fear I would recognize you. But fear not, Lavinia."

She was close to running away out of mortification.

"How did you know it was me?"

"I could identify that behind of yours anywhere."

"Are you confessing that you've been keeping an eye on my posterior?" She was livid, but strangely pleased. She was rather proud of her body and the prime shape she had kept it in.

"It wasn't deliberately done, I assure you."

"All that experience as society's most notorious rake has to give one some skills, I assume," she said as he led her through the waltz.

"Did you see Cassandra yet?"

"I think I saw someone who reminded me of her. Though so much time has passed that I could be entirely wrong."

"You didn't quite explain the other day. What precisely was the nature of your grouse against her?"

Lavinia looked down. "I couldn't tell you, sir, even if I wished to. It is too private and too scandalous."

"Did she hurt you?"

Lavinia was shocked at the tenderness in his voice. She hadn't thought him capable of that.

"Yes, she did. Very much," she said, just as softly.

"Forgive me for so insistently inquiring into a matter that is clearly so painful to you. You can tell me in your own time, but you don't have to."

"Thank you, sir. I would likewise not press you for your reasons for not wishing to marry her."

"My reasons are shamefully straightforward. It is a devious plan by my father to marry me to a fortune huntress so that I can spend the rest of my life being miserable with someone whom I can feel no passion for."

At the mention of passion, Lavinia's interest was quickened. "Do you expect passion in marriage, sir?"

"I don't expect it, but I wouldn't enter a marriage knowing it was never a possibility."

"What about Cassandra led you to believe that she's a fortune huntress, or that passion wouldn't be a possibility with her? I'm assuming you've met her only at Almack's."

"You know about Almack's?" he asked, not to snub her but because he was genuinely surprised. Governesses and servants knew of the polite society, but weren't aware of its private names or rules.

"One hears things, if one has a quick ear."

"You do, no doubt. So yes, I've met her only at masquerade balls, and honestly, I don't know what she looks like. I've seen likenesses, and she looks acceptable, though nothing out of the ordinary."

"The only thing out of the ordinary about her is her deviousness," Lavinia was quick to add.

"I believe you. Men and women of my station are raised to be polite snobs and follow the money. Most of us turn into scoundrels."

"Is that why you prefer the demi-monde and houses of ill-repute?"

It was Edmund's turn to blush. He wasn't a diffident man by any means, but the suddenness of Lavinia's conclusion caught him unawares. She was also a hundred percent correct.

"I do, madam. I would rather marry a kitchen maid, if she has the right sort of mind, than an heiress worth a hundred thousand pounds."

Lavinia was white with shock. "I understand no one knows it is you, but should you be uttering such scandalous statements when people are probably straining their ears to catch you in the act of saying something inappropriate?"

"My reputation wasn't built on saying appropriate things, Lavinia. I delight in shaking up the bon ton."

"What do you stand to lose if you just walk away from the marriage?"

"The privilege of being able to speak my mind to those I detest. If poor, I would be at their mercy."

Now that was a sentiment she could whole-heartedly agree with. Maybe they weren't as dissimilar as she had initially thought. They danced for a little longer, but in silence. It seemed as though the things worth saying had been spoken already.

Of course, she could always trust Templeton to shock her.

"Would you marry me, Lavinia?"

She felt as though she had walked into someone else's dream, probably Cassandra's. Edmund Templeton was proposing marriage? To her? After just being engaged to someone she loathed?

"Of course not, Mr. Templeton. How can I?"

"What's stopping you?"

She decided to play along. "To start with, the difference in our social positions. I'm just a governess, and you are heir to who knows how many thousands of pounds. Since you're the younger son, you would likely not get the estate. So you would be prudent to marry into money, to assure your continued financial security."

Edmund waltzed in thoughtful silence. "Let's say that this objection can somehow be removed, through a quirk of my own personality. I don't care much for money. Any other objections?"

"I don't wish to marry," she began. "Before starting as a governess, I was a nurse. I've seen too many women die painfully in childbirth. I have no wish to suffer that fate."

"I assure you that I would not make you bear children. I have no desire to sire heirs, since I would have no estate. Still other objections?"

So many, she wanted to say. My own past for one.

"You're proposing to me so that you don't have to marry Cassandra. That's not a very noble motive."

"And you might just accept me because you hate her and can't have her ordering you around here. I think we're evenly matched."

Lavinia had nothing to say to that. She hadn't had anything to drink, but she might as well have, since she was considering his proposal very seriously.

"Are there no other motives for your proposal beyond your current situation?"

"None that have occurred to me thus far. Though I must admit, your attractiveness certainly played its own part."

She was at a loss, yet again. How could his regard make her feel so unguarded? She knew that he hadn't fallen in love or something equally saccharine, then why was she so interested?

"So you want to escape an arranged marriage using another?"

"But I'm arranging the second one. You would agree that it makes all the difference."

"Mr. Templeton, this is entirely unexpected. You must give me a moment to compose myself before I take a decision."

"Under normal circumstances, I would not impose a limitation. But as you very well know, I must inform my father tonight, before the Wycliffs leave."

Under normal circumstances, he would not propose to me. She couldn't understand why the thought made her vaguely sad.

"Do you have an answer?" he asked gently, when she didn't say anything for a while.

"Yes. I will marry you, Mr. Templeton."

"Thank you," he said, pulling off his mask and flashing her a smile.

They had not even finished their step when there was a loud commotion from a corner of the ballroom.

"Oh, those damned villagers," Edmund said. "This is why I dislike public balls."

"It seems to be more serious than a usual drunken fight," she said.

"Whatever it is, my brother seems to be at the centre of it. I'll have to go and break it up. You wait here."

"I might be your fiancé, but I'm also a nurse. If people are injured, I need to be there."

Edmund gave her a resigned look, and took her by the hand.

Chapter 4

If she had been indignant at having to hold his hand as though she were a child, she saw its good sense now. The crush was maddening. Lords, villagers, ladies, common women...everyone was drunk, and had shed all inhibitions. Quite a few men tried to grab her in inappropriate places, and she had to kick many more out of her way.

Finally, when they reached the eye of the storm, they saw a very inebriated James Templeton attacking two villagers.

"You ungrateful swine! You dare come into my house and spread your filth!"

In response, a few villagers mumbled something and began to charge towards him.

"Leave him alone," Edmund shouted.

"We won't," the villager shouted back. "He's been trying to throw us out ever since the ball began."

"Come upstairs and we will settle it like gentlemen."

"But we aren't no genteel folks, my Lord," one of them shouted and turned on James.

Before Edmund and Lavinia could make sense of what was happening, someone had kicked James in the chest. He yowled in pain. They ran to his rescue, but were overpowered by the villagers, who were determined to take revenge on James. Something hard hit them and they both lost consciousness.

When Lavinia came to, she found herself on a bed she had never seen before. Edmund was lying next to her, still unconscious. She was about to jump to the worst conclusion and assume that he had seduced her, but the fact that both of them had clothes on belied that.

Her memory wasn't serving her at all. What was she doing there? And even more importantly, where were the others? Wasn't there a big ball underway?

And then it came rushing back. The masquerade ball. Templeton's proposal and her acceptance. The chaos. And the attack on James Templeton.

She felt a shiver; the room was unheated. She had to be in Courtney Hall, and this had to be some guest room or someone's bedroom. Whoever had rescued them from the mayhem had not thought too seriously about propriety, for else they would not have placed Edmund and her on the same bed.

Getting out of the bed gingerly, she slipped her shoes on. She managed to find her way to the ballroom somehow, but it was eerily deserted. Where was the Duke? And the Duchess? Were they also lying unconscious in some bedroom? She walked towards the main door. It was wide open. It was only then that she realized it was early morning. When she neared it, she could hear some voices outside. To her relief, it was the Duke.

"Your Grace, what is the matter? What happened at the ball?"

He turned to look at her. He looked wrecked.

Next to him, the Duchess stood, her face stained with tears.

"My son is dead," the Duke announced. "Murdered at the hands of the rioting villagers."

Lavinia went numb. She had seen the brutality of the fight firsthand, but she could still not believe it. "Where are all the servants, Your Grace? Why is no one attending to you?"

"They are all either asleep or alcohol-addled. I'm surprised you woke up."

She felt really sorry for the Duke. The poor man had lost his son mere hours ago, and without his knowledge, his younger son had become engaged to a governess of the house. She was suddenly filled with remorse.

"I will go indoors and see if I can find someone to help. Would you like me to take both of you indoors?"

"Thank you, Miss Lavinia. But Tilda and I would rather stay outside."

As she was walking along the hall, her first thought was Edmund. She had to wake him and tell him what had happened. What he had lost.

When she reached the room she had been asleep in, she found Edmund missing. She didn't want to be the one to break the awful news to him, but she also didn't want him to remain oblivious to the harsh reality.

She found him near the kitchens.

"Oh, Lavinia, thank the Lord! Where is everyone? Where have you been?"

Inhaling deeply, she related everything to him from the moment she had woken up in the room.

Edmund sat down, heart heavy with shock. He had never been particularly fond of his brother, but he had not been prepared for this. Rage mingled with helplessness as he rushed out of doors.

"Where are you going?"

"To kill those villagers!"

"But your father already sent them to prison."

"No matter. I will kill the rest of them."

"Edmund. You cannot kill all of them for what only a few of them did. I understand you're grieving, but you're going on a futile chase."

"I could've prevented this, Lavinia. I could've prevented this by not leaving him unguarded. Mother was worried the villagers might riot."

"There were guards on duty. Whatever happened, happened despite our best efforts. Please don't blame yourself."

She was hardly feeling on solid ground herself, but her priority was to comfort Edmund. Despite the circumstantial nature of their engagement, she began to feel more like his real fiancé with every minute that passed.

After awhile, everyone convened in the library. The Duke, the Duchess, Edmund, Clara (James' widow) and Lavinia.

"What happened after I lost consciousness, Father? I want all the details."

"I don't think you should be hearing the details at the moment, Mr. Templeton," Lavinia said. "It would do you more harm than good. You need to contain your nerves first."

"And I should listen to you because?"

"Because she is completely right," the Duke said. "Any exposure to traumatic details would only harm all of us. So let us stay as calm as we can, and decide what to do now."

Edmund looked as though he wanted to argue, but he looked too exhausted to. Lavinia wanted to reach out to him, but couldn't without disclosing her status to the entire family. She had no wish to impose that on any of them.

"The servants are gradually getting the house back in order. Lunch would be ready in a few hours, Albert just informed me. Miss Lavinia, I'm entrusting Henrietta completely to your charge. She's been given a sleeping draught, and when she wakes up, she will need all your help."

"Yes, Your Grace."

"Edmund, as my heir," the Duke continued as though it gave him pain to say it, "you will start overseeing the workings of the estate from this very day. Your conduct so far has not been above reproach, but the future of Courtney Hall and Yorkshire lies with you now. You will marry Miss Cassandra Wycliff as soon as the mourning period is over, without remonstrance, and the two of you will bear heirs as soon as feasible. I do not want the estate being entailed away to some hateful cousin."

"Yes, Father."

It was the first time anyone had seen Edmund so meek, but if the tragic loss of a brother doesn't humble you, then nothing would.

"The pain of losing James isn't going to dull anytime soon, but I would like to see the house and the estate to run uninterrupted," the Duchess added. "It is what James would've wanted as well."

"And needless to say, but Courtney Hall would be hosting no more public subscription balls. And no masquerade balls, however private."

The funeral for James was held the next day, with a sizeable attendance. The Wycliffs had come, no doubt to show their respects, but also to confirm their daughter's marriage to Edmund now that he was an even bigger prospect than before. Lavinia could only imagine Cassandra's glee.

The more she watched from behind the shadows, the more convinced she became that her one chance at a better life had just slipped out of her reach. She had even begun to like Edmund enough to make the prospect of marrying him not altogether horrible, but if she asked him to deliver on his promise now, it would lower him in his father's eyes considerably and perhaps ruin him for good.

So she decided to do the most graceful thing she could think of doing; she handed in her resignation to Lord Templeton, and left the house the very next morning. Her grief at leaving Henrietta behind was great indeed, but she was certain that the young woman would find many a suitable governess to guide her.

Chapter 5

When Edmund woke the next morning to the news that Lavinia had resigned, he could only blame himself. He had taken an innocent governess who was happy with her position, made her dream of a better station for his own selfish purposes and left her with no choice but to resign once his marriage became inevitable. Having always believed that his behaviour couldn't hurt anyone, he was faced with the realization that he had deeply wounded someone he was beginning to care about.

With only a few weeks to go before their wedding, he was being forced to spend an increasing amount of time in Cassandra's presence, and every moment spent with her was bringing her lower in his estimation. She was a dull, frivolous, mercenary woman, no different from everyone else. When he spoke to her, he couldn't stop thinking about Lavinia and how he could possibly atone for the way he had treated her. He had known precious little about where she had come from, and while he had tasked a couple of his servants to look for her, their efforts had been in vain. At a ball in London, he thought he spotted her, but then remembered that governesses didn't attend Almack's. Her absence had left him thoroughly puzzled, for while he knew he had been attracted to her, he wasn't prepared for the deluge of emotions that he was feeling now. He was even tempted to ask Cassandra what she knew of Lavinia, but couldn't risk breaking his promise to her. Unknown to anyone, Lavinia had gone back to her position as seamstress at Madam Brummell's in London. And because her life never quite tired of putting her in ironical positions, her first assignment was to help stitch Cassandra's wedding gown, which she was to take to Courtney Hall the day before the wedding.

She boarded the carriage that the Wycliffs had ordered, and set out for Yorkshire. Desperately not wanting to be recognized, she had covered her forehead with a veil and darkened her skin.

"Is Miss Wycliff here?" she asked Albert.

"Who is it, Albert?" Edmund asked from not very far away.

"It's Miss Wycliff's seamstress, come to deliver her wedding gown."

"Let her in, Miss Wycliff would be here in no time."

His voice was impassive, befitting the station he was now preparing for. It pained Lavinia to hear it, for she missed his old roguish disregard for rules. She wondered if showing herself would bring some sort of change in his countenance, but she didn't want to cause him undue pain.

Thanking Albert, she went inside the salon, where Cassandra was waiting for her.

"Edmund! Please don't leave yet. I want you to see the dress I've got made."

"Miss Wycliff, thank you but I have some important estate matters to attend to."

"The lady of the house insists, Your Grace," Lavinia said, without thinking. "It would be wise to humour her."

"Thank you, young lady," Cassandra said to her.

Lavinia heaved a sigh of relief, but looked at Edmund to gauge his reaction. She wasn't disappointed. He hadn't forgotten the sound of her voice, and his face went white as a sheet.

"Brenda!" Cassandra called to her lady's maid, "please carry this gown to my quarters."

"Cassandra, why don't you put it on and show me how it looks?" Edmund asked her.

"You really want to see? Don't you have estate matters to attend to now?"

"I do, but I'm getting married for the first time. So I wouldn't want to miss the little joys."

"As you say, future husband!" Cassandra said and departed with Brenda.

They were now left alone in the salon. Neither of them dared to say a word. Eventually, Lavinia broke the silence.

"My apologies for forcing my identity on you like that, but I really wanted to wish you the best."

"That was a tremendous risk. I'm shocked Cassandra didn't recognize you."

"No matter. My task is accomplished."

She was about to leave, when Edmund approached her and put his hand on her shoulder.

"I cannot let you slip out of my reach this time. You don't know how violently I've missed you," and before she knew it, his lips were on hers.

A thousand worries flashed through her mind, but Edmund's all-encompassing warmth made her forget them. In that moment, all she was aware of was the kiss.

"I'm terribly sorry, Lavinia. I've been most unfair to you. But know that my sentiments are sincere, more sincere than they've ever been."

"But what about your estate? And your father?"

"With you gone, I had a lot of time to think. And I've realized that I don't value the estate over my own happiness. This time, it's not about escaping an undesirable marriage, but choosing a desirable one."

Lavinia didn't dare to believe her ears. "Are you sure, Edmund?"

"Yes, my darling. Let's go and tell my father."

"Is there any chance he would agree?"

"Oh, I think you got the wrong impression. I'm not going in to ask for his permission. I'm merely going in to inform him."

"But you don't even know my full name."

"Isn't Lavinia Templeton good enough for you?"

She looked into his eyes, supremely apologetic. "No, not when your maiden name was Jacobina Wycliff."

Edmund had to sit down. Of all the possible connections between Lavinia and Cassandra, he couldn't have imagined this one.

"Oh Lord. Are you the Earl's illegitimate daughter?"

"No, I'm afraid. Cassandra is my legitimate younger sister."

"Then how did they cast you off?"

"It was Cassandra's doing. She had a liaison with an attractive footman at Windermere when we were fifteen. She became with child, planned a vacation with her friends and me to deliver the baby. We had been the closest of companions back then. However, when she got back and the county started to chatter, she convinced everyone that we had all gone there to help me deliver the baby and that I 'd had the liaison."

"And your parents believed her and exiled you."

"They had to exile someone, and I was easier to blame. There was no evidence but for the footman's word, and he had fled too long ago."

"I'm so sorry to hear this, Jacobina. But thank you for telling me. This can solve all our problems at once."

"How so? Wouldn't it add to your problems?"

"Fortunately, no, my darling. In our society, marrying an Earl's daughter with a rumoured scandalous past is far more respectable than marrying a governess."

"Father, I wish to talk to you. Most urgently."

"Certainly, Edmund," Lord Templeton said, "Why, it's Miss Lavinia! Welcome back!"

"I've come in to announce my engagement to Miss Wycliff."

"And your announcement is perfectly acceptable, and perfectly late."

"I don't suppose you follow what I'm saying, Father. I meant my engagement to Miss Jacobina Wycliff, Cassandra's older sister."

"Do you have any evidence of what happened, Miss Jacobina?" the Duke said, part amused, part skeptical.

"I do. The illegitimate child is the ward of the Marchioness of Exeter. I had delivered him to her personally all those years ago."

"But who would believe you?"

"Whoever would care to look closely at my family and me."

"But I wouldn't be amenable to this marriage unless we can convincingly discredit Cassandra and have her fortune transferred to you."

"Your Grace, your offer of a touching family reunion is very welcome, but I don't think we have time for that. The wedding is tomorrow."

The Duke looked thoughtful. "I might have some standing with the Marquis. But these are extremely sensitive matters. Are you certain of the parentage of the Marchioness' ward?"

"Upon my word, sir."

"Edmund, you must know that I wouldn't have done this, but you've acquitted yourself rather honorably in the last few months. The estate has become more profitable than it was under James or under me. So I'm going to do all I can to ensure your marriage Miss Wycliff."

"That would be the first fatherly thing you've done for me, I thank you. Though this time, please be sure you're choosing the right Miss Wycliff to saddle me with."

"Jacobina! Where did she enter the stage from?" a very livid Countess Cumbria asked Lord Templeton.

"I'm afraid she's been a major player from the very beginning," Edmund said.

"I will not let this happen," Cassandra said. "I will prove her wrong."

"Unfortunately, Miss Wycliff, the Marchioness of Exeter has assured me that she would testify in court about the parentage of young Victor."

"That gutter snake!" Cassandra screeched.

"I'm very sorry to have wasted your time, Cassandra. Believe me, it was unwillingly done," Edmund said.

"Countess, if you would like to meet your daughter and apologize for the past five years, she would be available at Courtney Hall," the Duke said before parting.

"I have no wish to talk to her. She just ruined my daughter's prospects."

"Your daughter ruined them herself at age fifteen. Jacobina was merely caught between your blind love for Cassandra and Cassandra's selfishness. The inheritance, however, can be claimed in a court of law, which is a route I do not wish to go. So even if you don't wish to talk to her, please be sure of sending the documentation along with a servant."

Chapter 6

Jacobina could scarcely believe her ears.

"Are you sure Cassandra and Mother have been sufficiently cowed?" she asked Edmund as she held the documents to her inheritance of ten thousand pounds.

"It would be the word of a Duke and a Marchioness against a Countess'. I don't think any Court would believe the latter."

"Something about this easy victory doesn't feel right to me, Edmund."

"Put your mind at peace. We've done nothing wrong in getting your rightful inheritance and name back."

While she wasn't really convinced, she nodded, hoping the spectre of Cassandra was gone from her life for good.

"Father, I don't agree with your proposal for avoiding a scandal in the bon ton. There has to be another way."

"I want the welfare of the Templeton family as badly as you do. Trust me, if there was another way, I would've found it. But you really must not lift Jacobina's bridal veil."

"Aren't you worried about the kind of speculation that would set off?"

"A mysterious bride is better than a ruined bride, don't you think?"

Edmund was livid, but he was beginning to see his father's reasoning. The Edmund-Cassandra engagement had been publicized so much that revealing another bride all of a sudden would shock society. But if they broke the news gradually, starting with small parties and introducing Jacobina into polite society one family at a time, they would have an easier time accepting that she had been Edmund's intended all along, and the whole affair with Cassandra had just been a misunderstanding.

But Cassandra hadn't been born to just sit back while her hated sister walked away with everything she had been working towards. She had lost out on becoming a Duchess by a hair's breadth, just because the vile Jacobina had somehow ensnared the Duke's family.

She called her groom to arrange for a chaise and four, and set off for London, where the Templetons and Jacobina were going to solemnize the marriage. On the morning of the wedding, she disguised herself as a common dairy maid, and proceeded to the church. She meant to catch Jacobina before she could enter church, knowing that her quarters would be heavily guarded.

The wedding was to be a private affair, with only the closest friends of the Templetons in attendance. They were especially conscious of the presence of any ill-meaning Wycliffs, and Jacobina was to remain under a veil throughout.

Jacobina's carriage had just pulled over preparing to make way to the church. A woman in a beautiful black dress with matching veil neared the carriage chanting something rather low. Jacobina leaned in to understand the jibberish which sounded like "may this be well with your soul". suddenly, a jagged knife began slashing from her right ear to her lower throat. The motion of the woman's arm changed to a downward stabb. Jacobina was stabbed four times in the stomach.

"Jacobina! NO!", Edmund had no time to react. Blood was all over the carriage and sprayed all over his wedding clothes.

"She is going to carry scars and the stitches should hold. By the grace of God the cuts aren't very deep, or she would've got infected and died," the physician said. "I recommend rest for two weeks."

"This has to be the work of the Wycliffs," Edmund said to the Duke. "We must have them imprisoned for attempted murder."

"But we would need evidence. All we know is that someone clad in black attacked her."

"It can wait then. My immediate priority is to have Jacobina relocated to a safe destination."

"And the wedding?"

"I think our only safe bet is a private exchange of vows in front of the priest, right here."

The priest was called and the wedding solemnized in Jacobina's bedchamber, as soon as she was feeling herself. She could still not be relocated immediately, and the two weeks of rest that the physician had recommended proved to be the hardest of Edmund's life. He barely slept, standing constant guard in her room and attending to every need of hers.

She would often look at her badly scarred neck in the mirror and despair that Edmund would not find her attractive anymore. But he would reassure her that it wouldn't ever be the case.

"If anything, the scars would remind me what my love cost you. I'm not so ungrateful a man as to lessen my regard for you over something that inconsequential."

She would blush, and that would be the end of that.

"Are Scotland Yard any closer to guessing who it was?" she would always ask. And the answer was always No.

"Till when must we live thus cautious of every movement?"

"I don't know, Jacobina. I hate it. But I'm looking forward to our trip to Scotland."

"How would we make the trip without falling prey to the same dangers? At least in the house, we can have numerous guards."

"We would travel in an enormous entourage of hardened warriors. I think we should be quite safe."

Jacobina didn't look very reassured, but she knew that staying in London wasn't safe at all.

The two weeks did pass, and it was time for their departure.

"Usually, newlyweds don't take so many people on their first holiday together," she said dryly, remarking on the hundred or so people traveling behind them. "Imagine the utter lack of privacy."

"I promise you, my darling, we would be left quite alone once we reach our Scotland home. And I hope that the peace there would compensate for all the chaos we've been seeing ever since the day that wretched engagement was decided."

"Do you think your Father feels to blame for it all? Had he never betrothed you to Cassandra, none of this would've happened."

"I think he does. That would explain his ready assistance in enabling me to marry you. He does care about me, after all."

"He's a wonderful father. Not quite the hard-hearted man you portrayed him as."

"We discovered his obliging side together, Jacobina. I had no way of knowing it earlier."

Their Scottish home was a three day journey away, and they reached there extremely exhausted but glad at having made it without any trouble. The house they had rented was luxurious and Jacobina felt that since they were going to stay there for a long time, it made sense to furnish it as fully as possible.

"Darling, I hope you're ready for a wonderful holiday," he said, lifting her in his arms.

"I'm not sure. I still had a few questions."

Edmund looked a little worried, but the mischief in her eyes set him at ease.

"What made you realize you could tolerate being married to me?"

"I must credit your utter unwillingness to hold me in awe, which is what I've been used to. I felt a kinship, for I feel the same disregard for the conventions of polite society."

She was quiet for a few moments.

"And you?"

"I think it was your honesty. Even when you were making that proposal of convenience to me, you did not try to make it palatable by adding any romance. I knew then that I could trust you to keep your word."

"I was amazed when you told me the truth about your identity. I think that's when I knew that you had implicit trust in me."

"And you would be right, because I had planned on never disclosing it to you."

"You were going to marry me as Lavinia?"

"Yes. Would it have made such a difference?"

"You would not have been attacked and suffered so much pain, so it might've been the better option."

"But I couldn't continue to deceive you, not when you had been so honest with me. So maybe this was the only option available to us."

"I'm glad it led us here," he said, and pulled her into a kiss.

"About that, there can never be any doubt."

Epilogue

Within six months, Edmund and Jacobina were able to return to Courtney Hall. Cassandra's groom confessed to bringing her to London on the night before the wedding, and it was finally proved that she had made the attempt on Jacobina's life. She was sentenced to imprisonment. Unfortunately, Lord Templeton passed away around the same time in a bout of rheumatic fever.

After the funeral services for Lord Templeton, Edmund and Jacobina took their places as the Duke and Duchess at Courtney Hall, with the blessings of the people they were going to be responsible for.